The Tickle Bug

Written by

Gary DeFlorio

and illustrated by

Patricia Weber-Rohrer

The Tickle Bug, a book from the delightful series "Adventures with Papa"

Printed in the United States of America
First Printing, 2013

ISBN-13: 978-1484189351
ISBN-10: 1484189353

Co-Published by Hear The Visions, LLC
and The Glu Group, LLC
Sylvan Lake, MI 48320

Dedicated to…

My kids and grandkids who were on the receiving end of Dad's/Papa's silly bedtime stories for over a decade. And especially to my daughter Taylor who encouraged me to start putting them down on paper - I love you with my whole heart.

God, who provided me with the perseverance, patience, and people to make this happen.

Danny Frushour, Laura Schorn, Colleen Benn, and especially Pat Weber-Rohrer whose gift of art made a simple idea truly come alive.

My readers who I hope will seek to capture a tickle bug of their very own.

    Once upon a time in a little house in the country there lived two little girls, Tabitha and Lydia. Behind the girls' house, as far as one could see, was what everyone called the Big Woods. The girls could not wait for the day when they would be able to go exploring there.

One summer evening as Mother tucked them into bed, the girls could hardly sleep. They hoped and prayed that tomorrow would be a beautiful day because Papa, their grandfather, was coming to spend the day with them and take them on a fun adventure. Finally, Tabitha and Lydia fell fast asleep.

Before long, they awoke and rushed to the window. It was a bright sunny day!

The smell of their favorite breakfast slowly drifted up the stairs and into their bedroom as the little girls hurried to get dressed and make their beds.

"Mmmm. Mother is making chocolate chip pancakes," said Lydia.

"And sausage too!" exclaimed Tabitha.

After breakfast, the girls helped their mother clean up the kitchen and then sat down to wait for Papa to arrive.

It wasn't long before Papa could be seen strolling up the lane to their front door.

He was carrying something strange on his back!

The girls greeted Papa at the door and laughed as Papa said, "My hugs will squish you like blueberries!"

After the hugs and kisses were done, Lydia asked about the hump that had been on his back.

"It's a backpack, and you need to make your favorite sandwiches, snacks, and drinks and put them into it because we are going into the Big Woods on a hiking adventure!"

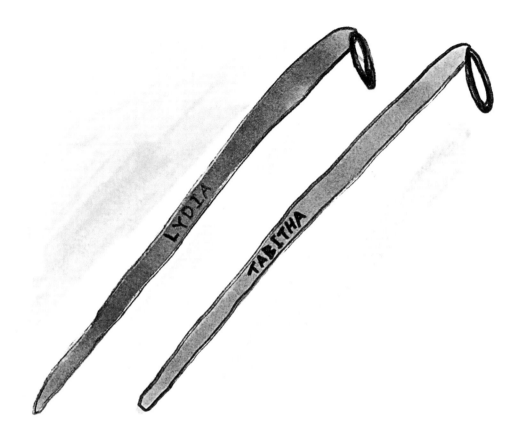

Before heading out into the woods, Papa gave each girl a long walking stick he had made in his workshop just the day before.

"These are important for hiking in the woods," Papa told them as they began their journey.

The little group walked along the path to a point where it finally reached the woods. Lydia looked up through the trees as they went along.

"Papa, look! The sun is blinking off and on!" she exclaimed excitedly.

Along the path in the woods, the girls and their grandpa passed rivers and streams, tall hills, and deep valleys. They heard the birds chirping in the trees and the frogs croaking on their water lily pads, while the crickets sang as they passed by.

Papa showed the girls how to use their walking sticks to poke around the weeds for snakes and turtles and other little creatures that lived and played at the water's edge.

After a while, the group came to a small clearing in the woods.

"I'm getting hungry, Papa," said Tabitha.

"Me too," Lydia added.

"All right," Papa told them, "we can have our lunch here by the creek."

The three of them wolfed down sandwiches and juice and lay back in the soft green grass to rest for a while.

All was quiet as they relaxed and enjoyed the warm afternoon sun on their faces.

They watched the clouds move slowly through the sky. Tabitha liked to pick out shapes of animals and other stuff in the clouds. "That one looks like a dog," she said pointing across the sky.

"And I see one that looks like a shoe!" Lydia piped in happily.

Suddenly Papa sat up straight and cried, "Look! There's one, right there on the end of the branch!"

Lydia and Tabitha turned quickly to see what Papa was pointing at.

They looked at the bush and up and down the branches.

Nothing was there.

"Ssshhh," whispered Papa quietly, "you must be very quiet and remain perfectly still if you want to catch the bug."

"What kind of bug is it?" asked Tabitha.

Slowly Papa turned toward the girls and whispered, "It's a tickle bug."

Neither Lydia nor Tabitha had ever heard of a tickle bug.

"Do tickle bugs bite?" asked Lydia.

"No," replied Papa with a small smile.

He took a couple of quiet steps toward the bush, and with one fast swipe of his hand, Papa grabbed at the end of the bush!

For a few moments, everyone froze as the girls
wondered if their grandpa had caught the tickle
bug.   Then Papa threw his head back, and his
shoulders shook as he laughed! He began to sing
and dance, and soon Tabitha and Lydia joined in.
They laughed and sang and danced around the
small clearing by the creek.

Finally, Papa stopped to catch his breath. Falling to the ground, he suddenly began to swing his arms around wildly!

"The tickle bug is trying to escape!" he shouted. He gasped and lunged toward Tabitha. "It's under your arm!" he cried as he reached under her arm to retrieve the bug.

"That tickles!" she giggled as Papa chased the tickle bug back and forth from under her right arm to her left.

As Papa continued to try to catch the tickle bug that was jumping on Tabitha, all three of them were laughing. Every time he got close to catching it, the bug got away! Harder and harder, they laughed until Tabitha couldn't breathe.

Now the bug was jumping on Lydia and it landed beneath her ribs! Papa tried to pinch it, which made Lydia laugh even harder.

"Let me go, please! I can't breathe!" She cried. "Stop! Stop!"

Soon the laughter stopped, and the girls were quiet. Papa told them that the tickle bug was gone. It had made one last jump onto a branch and scampered up the tree.

As the sun sank lower in the sky, the three hikers began their journey home. Walking and skipping down the path in the woods, the girls talked of their adventure with the tickle bug.

Up and down the hills, they trudged, past the rivers and streams to where the path narrowed and then disappeared into the lane that led to their house.

As Papa waved goodbye to the girls, they wondered how long it would be before he took them on another adventure.

Calling back to them, Papa said, "I'll be back soon, and I'll make our next adventure as fun as this one!"

And they believed him.